FRAGMENTS

FRAGMENTS

From the world of **C. Jinarajadasa**

Compiled by
Elithe Nisewanger

This publication made possible with the assistance of the Kern Foundation.
The Theosophical Publishing House
Wheaton, Ill. / Madras, India / London, England

A Quest original, 1980, published by the Theosophical Publishing House, a department of the Theosophical Society in America. Inquiries for permission to reproduce all or portions of this book should be addressed to Quest Books, 306 West Geneva Road, Wheaton, Illinois 60187.

Library of Congress Cataloging in Publication Data

Jinarajadasa, Curuppumullage, 1875-1953
  Fragments: from the world of Jinarajadasa
  (Quest Books)
   1. Theosophy—Collected works. I. Nieswanger,
Elithe. II. Title.
BP525.J49   1979   212′.52   79-3663
ISBN 0-8356-0533-7

Printed in the United States of America

CONTENTS

SOURCES OF QUOTATIONS

FOREWORD

When the renowned Theosophist, C. W. Leadbeater, was invited to go to England to be resi-
dent tutor for A. P. Sinnett's son, Denny, he
took with him a 13-year-old Sinhalese boy—C.
Jinarajadasa—to share the lessons. The deep
spiritual potential of this lad was obvious to
Leadbeater and he was determined to provide
him with this learning opportunity.

The gifted boy excelled under C.W.L.'s tute-
lage, and his European education fitted him for
his future service to The Theosophical Society.
During this early period of training, he trav-
elled extensively throughout Europe. He developed multilingual abilities which prepared him to
work easily with the many different national Sec-
tions of the Society.

Young Jinarajadasa's voyage to England was
the beginning of a sixty-four-year relationship
between him and The Theosophical Society. He
was elected International President of the Society in 1946 and he held that office until his death
in 1953.

Brother "Raj", as he was affectionately known, inspired people. His enthusiasm for life clearly shines through his many literary works, as do his deep knowledge of, and appreciation for, the arts, and his intense devotion to theosophy.

These *Fragments* have been gathered together with love by Elithe Nisewanger, who served as his secretary while he was President of the Society. We earnestly hope that this small collection of some of his finest thoughts will, in turn, inspire you. They are, indeed, "fragments" of his wisdom, yet, paradoxically, each is a "whole".

R.S.

1. THEOSOPHY

WHAT is termed *Theosophy* today is an aggregate of the best thought which is found, in part, in every religion, philosophy and mysticism. It is based on the facts of Nature, and the facts of the supernatural, of mysticism, of psychological states are considered as much the data of knowledge as any data discovered in scientific laboratories. It is a body of philosophical truths to examine critically, not to accept blindly on what another may proclaim.

THEOSOPHY is not merely a beautiful intellectual philosophy, but it rouses in us a power to call out the latent divinity within.

THEOSOPHY is not merely a group of fascinating ideas; each of its truths is a law of nature, that is, reveals the way that Nature is at work, thus truth becomes a power in the character. To see life as a whole is one of the effects of its study, and with a widening of the mind's horizon there spring up new wells of inspiration.

THEOSOPHY teaches that man is dual, that he has a body made of matter, but is an immortal soul which can never cease to exist. The mortal part, that body of flesh and blood, certainly is related to the highest animals, but the body is not the true man. He is the invisible, immortal soul, an emanation from God and, therefore, fundamentally divine. His body perishes, but not his memory, his consciousness, his affections, for all these are part of him as a soul.

THEOSOPHY is a statement of the laws discovered by the mind of man when investigating the manifestations of the Divine Mind. It, therefore, deals with reality.

THE theosophical conception is that the universe and its organisms do not come about merely as the result of Nature's experiments and chance variations, but that from the beginning there is a divine plan for evolution, and that no new type appears which was not intended to appear.

THEOSOPHISTS who desire to share their discoveries with others will help, not by giving them truths external to themselves, but by *awakening* them to those truths which reside in them. There must be an appeal not only to the mind but also to the intuition.

Two objectives which stand out in our work as Theosophists are, first, to understand the Wisdom ourselves, and second, to apply it in order to bring about great changes in ourselves and in the lives of all men and in the world.

To understand the Divine Plan which is the power behind evolution, and to hasten the realization of that Plan are the two main objectives of Theosophists.

As practical Theosophists, our way is not so much to try to convert a person as to *remind* him of the truth and awaken the wisdom which is within himself.

It is a fundamental axiom in Theosophy that God, Who is the Perfect, the Omnipotent, the Omniscient, and the utterly Free, dwells within us. But we are as if bound in chains, still in search of wisdom, freedom, and perfection.

The whole purpose of the message of Theosophy is to show that what the greatest of mankind has achieved shall one day be the achievement of every human being.

2. ELDER BROTHERS

THE Masters of the Wisdom are those souls who in the evolutionary process have passed beyond the stage of man to the next higher, that of the Adept. As a man becomes Adept he ceases to be merely an item in the evolutionary process, and appears as a master and director of that process, under the supervision of a mighty consciousness called the Logos. These agents of the Logos guide and direct the process in all its phases in the evolution of life and form on land and sea; they direct the rise and fall of nations; they ever reveal the Wisdom to guide mankind.

THE Masters of the Wisdom direct the rise and fall of continents; guide the struggle for existence in Nature; watch and guide every development in all its kingdoms, with the one aim of so molding the forces of life that all may swiftly carry out God's Plan of evolution. So too in the life of men, they guide the building of civilizations; they send to each nation those souls through whom they can give that culture necessary for its role in the drama of nations; they inspire the unselfish work of statesmen, teachers, poets, scientists and artists; they use also the selfishness and wrongdoing of men to destroy, so that later they may build still better.

It is to bear the burdens of humanity, and for this alone that the Elder Brothers of our race, the Masters of the Wisdom, live and work. If you desire to draw near to them, to be led to life Eternal, you must learn to bear the burdens of others, to share in their joys, and see that no act of yours adds to the sum total of pain in the world.

The greatness of the Master lies in the fact that in his vision of us he lifts us to where he stands, and indeed calls on us to be like him, and that his call gives us mystically an assurance that we, too, shall succeed. We have little realization that he has lived a perfect life only in order that he might be a pattern to us.

A HUMAN soul who has realized his own divinity and come to perfection, as we shall all come, goes on still further in the unfoldment of his divinity, and makes a far-reaching offering of love, of suffering and of devotion, with the object of standing for mankind as an exemplar and a mediator; he brings down into his own nature the indescribable glories of the Divine, and then, veiling these glories, reveals them to mankind.

A MASTER of the Wisdom is a perfect mirror of the Divine Thought, a flawless conductor of the Divine Will.

A KIND word, a smile, a beautiful thought, a deep sense of devotion, and very many seemingly small things add to the joy of the world. If we so create joy in His name, we shall find that with each little joy created there comes a fuller realization of the Master's presence.

A MASTER loves all men, but the individual must *make* the reason for being taken as an apprentice or disciple, his nature must be such that

he can share the Master's work and burden.
Therefore, the aspirant must first possess some
capacity of heart and mind developed in the service of man, he must be an idealist, willing to
suffer for his ideals if necessary.

THE Brotherhood of the Masters of the
Wisdom stands midway between God's life and
love, and the life of Nature and of man. They
work in ways visible and invisible, and it is the
privilege of those who so determine to be en-
rolled as Their servants and helpers.

THE Adepts of the Great White Brotherhood
work in true hierarchical order, according to their
qualifications, each having his work in a particular department of the Plan of the Logos.

THERE is only one way to find the Master, and
that is by first finding our own special work.
When one knocks at His door with the first fruits
of the harvest of work, the door swings open to
reveal visions of greater service still, but not
necessarily a vision of the Master.

THE Adept is past any need of reincarnation, he has already gained all the experiences which civilization can give him. Yet many an Adept reincarnates among men to be a guide and law-giver.

AN ideal is the first glimpse of the Master, who is a gateway to the Highest.

THE major part of the Master's work is in the invisible worlds, for the major part of Nature and of each soul is in those realms, and it is there that he brings down the vitality they need in order to grow and evolve. The Master is a direct channel of God's life.

THE consciousness of the Elder Brethren embraces all humanity, and since they labor to achieve the plan of evolution, no ultimate failure is possible for mankind, although they are constantly hindered in their work by the selfishness and unwillingness of men.

3. BROTHERHOOD

IF the work the few are doing represents the fulfilment of humanity's needs, then the World-Spirit, or the Time-Spirit, aids them. I hold that Brotherhood has a great creative role to accomplish in the building of the better civilization for which we long.

To give yourself utterly in self-sacrifice and service is to imitate God Himself.

I CONSIDER it the duty of everyone of goodwill to give all possible aid to make brotherhood an active principle in our international, national and civic life.

WE must renounce our individualism and discover a joy in working with others for a common purpose; it is the giving of ourselves that is far more important than any other giving.

OUR work is to proclaim brotherhood, not as an ideal, as some beautiful dream born in the imaginations of men, but as a reality, as a law of Nature.

GOD creates worlds and peoples them with His creatures, raises continents and destroys them, builds civilizations and humbles them to dust in order that men may learn the lessons of service and self-sacrifice, so that we may become channels of His highest life.

A MAN'S usefulness must be judged less from the abstract standpoint of usefulness towards the cosmos at large, and more from the standpoint of his direct use or service to his fellowmen.

IT is distinctly better to turn one's back on the things one hopes for in a distant future, in order to do some act of service before one here and now.

THE ideal of Brotherhood is waiting for its time to reveal its grandeur and to become the driving power in the imaginations of all men.

WHEN individuals meet together for a common work, each releases in the other some strength and some understanding which were not manifest before.

IT is by appealing to the divine within each that we shall become brothers.

4. THE DIVINE IN MAN

MAN is fundamentally beautiful and perfect, but as a *fragment* of divinity. It is because he does not realize his wonderful nature that he allows himself to be led astray by his passions, his ambitions, by the selfish and evil forces in the world. He is a slave to the senses of his lower self, because he is not yet awake as a soul. The eternal danger which threatens man's happiness is self-absorption; let a man but turn outwards to dedicate himself to a noble, unselfish work, and then he breaks away the chains which bind and imprison his divinity.

EVERY karmic difficulty, every pain and trouble, is not intended merely to "pay a debt to karma", to restore the universal equilibrium which has been disturbed by our actions, but all of them have also the purpose of drawing out of us the Divine nature within us.

THE supreme fact we must learn to understand is that man is not just a creature of flesh and bone, of many evil passions and emotions and a few virtues; there exists in him a spirit, tender and beautiful, waiting for release.

OUR true life begins when we work to carry forward the Plan of the Logos, to feel His thought, emotion, and will flaming in us, and to go out into the world energized by our own divinity and help to make His world perfect.

MEN are like prisoners, bound by the chains of ignorance, and our task is to release them from their bondage, to release the divinity within.

WHAT we find beautiful in any thing or in any event is only the beauty of the Divine Mind mirroring Itself in that thing and event.

TO be spiritual is a matter of looking into the hearts of men, sharing their joys and anguishes, and feeling that you can strengthen the weak and purify the muddy and ugly places of the world.

THE work of science of linking nation to nation has been a work of linking materially; science has not linked the nations spiritually in friendship.

So transmute your whole nature from day to day, from year to year, that you become dead to matter, for you have transformed matter into spirit.

5. THE CHILD

THE child can tell us of the mysteries of life when we study him as he is revealing himself, when we observe, understand and allow him to experiment with the apparatus provided for him. As we help the child to unfold, he helps us to unfold, just as the sun helps the bud to blossom.

SOME are old souls with great experiences and capacities, others are young souls, beautiful in nature but with undeveloped faculties. The child must not be forced to fit into a particular educational curriculum, but be guided to express itself, to find out quickly what contribution the soul desires to give to human welfare.

TO work to make children happy, as flowers are in the sunshine, is one method of assisting them to commune with the Great Teacher.

IT is of the greatest importance that everything which the child sees, hears or touches should have a quality of beauty about it, for the true purpose of teaching a child is to make him understand life as a great process in which he must take his part as a creator. Make a child sensitive to beauty, and he will become gradually more and more intuitive.

THE liberation of the soul of the child means not so much to teach him facts he does not know or does not want to know, but to lead into expression that which he knows *already* as an eternal soul.

IF only we know how to love children, at least know how to look at them in wonder and with eager desire to understand them, then God is very near.

IF the child does anything that is against *our* convenience, we promptly assume the child is doing wrong. It does not occur to us to ask if what the child is doing or not doing is right according to *his* standard of convenience.

THE child has come to earth from a happy place, the invisible world. He is born with a purpose as a soul, and it is necessary first to arouse in him an enthusiasm for the work he is to do, by making the home life and school life as full of happiness, love and beauty as possible, in order to remind him of the heaven whence he has come.

IF only we will help our children to be intuitive, then as they grow they will achieve where we have failed. The facts for their minds must be carefully selected and set in a framework of beauty.

EVERY thought, good or bad, every emotion, happy or unhappy, in parents, teachers, or anyone in close contact with a child, affects that child, no, rather, *infects* the child, because the subconscious self of a child is much more sensitive than that of an adult.

THE phrase "my child" gives parents no right over the destiny of the child, but only the privilege of helping in the evolution of a brother-soul.

Always the child needs to be surrounded by the right environment, be provided with an emotional and mental atmosphere that will foster the good tendencies from the past, and receive the treatment and training that will develop the sensitiveness of his higher nature.

I WOULD like to inscribe on the wall of every teachers' training school, "He who does not know how to love, cannot be a successful teacher."

IN molding the child's character, far more influential for good or evil are the thoughts of *others* which surround the child; it is far more influenced by what is *not* said and what it does *not* hear.

6. THE ARTIST

THE Great Artist dwells within us, not only outside us; what He does, that can we also. The creative artists of every nation are His chosen band of prophets, but since His nature is in each of us, somewhere in us too an artist is hidden—an artist in words, in humble ways of service, in great endurance and perfect heroism.

The artist is he who takes life as it comes, and transforms it till it reveals a hidden glory.

ART is an expression of the way in which the soul reacts to life with the intuition, a more complete understanding than we have so far realized through our emotions and our intellect.

THE art of any particular artist lies in the manner in which he reacts to the universe, through his intuition.

THE artist belongs to the totality of life—but his message is not to the universe in the abstract, it is distinctly to mankind as a whole. The creation of the artist is his own, but through it he appeals to the infinite faculty of dreaming, which is inseparable from the inmost heart of man.

IT is art which molds the soul of a people, creates and civilizes. It awakens the hidden best in the individual. When each responds to the message of life which art can give, he is a bigger individual, he is a more powerful dynamo of the forces of life.

IT is the function of the artist to see that human nature is not debased by trivialities, but to give expression to a certain tone, an element of good taste, that quality of the inner soul which knows instinctively the good from the bad, an imitation from a true creation of beauty, and has an inborn awareness of what is the best.

THE artist is he who takes hold of the forces of life and molds them anew. He uses his craft to grasp the root-material of life in order to fashion it into a thing of beauty, which then reflects the world as Idea. Every great artist is a vortex of life's forces, and the more he dominates and then reshapes them, the greater is he as an artist.

POETRY, sculpture, song, dance, music, architecture are all so many magic doors which open for us new regions of life, windows through which to look at a larger and more beautiful world, the world of our eternity.

ARTISTS belong to the humanity of intuition, they try to see life from the center, not from the circumference.

A GENIUS is a soul who is especially endowed with a sense of the creative power which is God, and which he has labored to develop through many lives.

To create artistically we must discover ourselves for awhile in a new role, as life's spectator and not its actor, as the immortal soul and not the perishable body.

EVERY artist, whether a sculptor, a landscape painter or a musician, chisels, paints, or composes *ideas*, not merely objects.

ALL branches of art should have an intensely ethical meaning, a direct message to mankind. It is only when the ethical concepts are felt extensively that we can have a really great era of art.

IF the artist is to create something which is to last for eternity, then he must find serenity among his ideas, be certain as to what he is himself and what is the purpose of the world.

Everything that the artist is, as an individual, is reflected in the thing he creates.

ESPECIALLY are art and religion inseparable. Almost all periods of artistic creation have arisen only when there have been great spiritualizing influences from religion.

HOWEVER small be the size of the work the true artist creates, there is in that creation something of the totality of the universe.

THE artist's reaction is not completely emotional, nor completely mental; he is experimenting with a new type of reaction to life.

BEFORE the artist can create, the outer universe must pour in through his senses in a larger measure than with ordinary man, he must have a keener, more delicately organized sensitiveness, but he must transform, not merely reproduce; he has to transform what he sees with the faculties of the emotions, the mind, the imagination, the intuition, the Spirit itself.

IT is for art to show us that there is a way to live, not in time but in eternity. Art is one way of giving, and to give is to live.

THE mysterious forces of life, which flow through all men, are utilized by the artist to shape the crude material of life into an aspect of the beautiful.

ALL the happiness, power and inspiration which we need are within us. We do not ordinarily find them, because we live in two worlds, an outer and an inner world, but the artist unites the two.

7. THE GREAT PLAN

IT is the One Life which manifests through the activities of men, and all the activities which have been developed in civilization are necessary in the Divine Plan. Men's natures have to be developed emotionally, mentally and spiritually, and one method of this growth is their collective activity in various spheres. In the evolution of humanity the faculties of all, good and bad, are used for gaining greater capacities and bringing high spirituality to all work.

IF we have a glimpse of the world as a great Idea, if we have seen the pattern, sensed something of the operation of the Plan, then we can know that it is working out in our lives, despite obstacles, failures and disappointments. We begin to have half-glimpses of the gods that we shall be when we shall have ceased to be the half-gods that we are at present.

THE purpose of life is not contemplation but action, and each action should be so guided by understanding that it fits in harmoniously with the divine Plan of evolution. The more a soul cooperates with that Plan, the happier, wiser, and more glorious it becomes.

THE Architect of the universe is not one who built once upon a time, but He is constantly constructing, destroying and reconstructing as He builds the perfect universe through the myriad souls who form mankind.

EVOLUTION is the picture of the organization of forms from the simple to the complex, from the indefinite to the definite, always arranging in such a way that more complex forms of life, essence, and reaction can manifest. It is a drawing out of something which is present already, not creating something new; each individual or thing is unreleased divinity.

THERE is the necessity for the discovery by man of his immortality, his deathlessness even while living in a form, a frame that dies.

WHAT is man's growth but a transmutation of experience, so as to ascend slowly stage by stage to release more of the Self, more understanding of life, more joy in living, more self-sacrifice.

To one who knows, or even senses, the Is-To-Be there is no death, but only life always, ever-striving to reveal lovelier splendors, and using as its tools matter, form, growth, decay, dissolution and rebirth in that framework of the unreal which we call days and nights.

THERE is a purpose in the universe which is molding good to better, and better to best. All things feel this growth into a larger life; at their root is a natural desire for more life, light and joy.

LIKE as the bud is urged from within to unveil its beauty and become the flower, so is life striving from within to unfold greater wisdom, strength and beauty. The only true happiness for men comes from helping life, in all its expressions, to reveal what is as yet unrevealed of its hidden glory.

It is only because God is immanent in the atom that the atom has substance and energy; it is the immanence of God in Nature which alone makes evolution possible.

THE universe is a revelation of the Logos, but it is not static; it unfolds its hidden divinity as the ages pass, and this is the soul of the fact of evolution.

THE process of evolution is the unfoldment of capacity, of beauty, of virtue, all of which reside in the universe from the beginning.

It is not by a miracle that we shall become perfect; perfection is a natural process intended by God so that by means of the experiences of many lifetimes of good and evil, joy and pain, selfishness and self-sacrifice the soul may grow purposefully, not blindly.

THERE is not one of us but is a genius unreleased, and though it takes ages before one inhibiting factor after another, of our own making,

is removed at the end of the ages, we shall all
stand forth visibly as what we always were invisi-
bly—sons of God and partakers of His glory.

HE serves evolution best who helps the Divine
Life to move more swiftly in its upward way.

WHEN you have trained yourself to see the pattern behind the Great Plan and its operation,
then you can see the fact of the world as Will, as
the great Sacrifice, an offering of God.

THE Is-To-Be is ever with us, if only we could
be aware of that fact. The only way to it is ever to
seek the highest.

THERE is no great or small in Nature's laws;
each is a center in the whole circle of the being
and the becoming.

WHEN with a trained imagination the soul
broods over the story of its sorrows and failures,
and sees rising from their lurid flames the arche-

type of what it shall become, then naught remains but to be one with it, in happiness and in misery, in victory and in defeat.

To Him, in whose nature is all the wisdom attainable by men, there is no division of events into secular or religious, earthly or heavenly. Each event is an occurrence according to God's Plan, and in its very happening reveals a little more of the hidden beauty and majesty of that Plan.

So long as we live on earth, a Yonder in the invisible worlds is always tugging to draw us back to its own sphere. Thus, it is that when our imagination has behind it the pressure of past longings for truth, love or beauty, we begin to contact the world of becoming.

THE question whether or not there is a Creator can only really be solved by each individual for himself, as the consciousness expands and he perceives all the facts of evolution and growth before him.

8. REINCARNATION AND KARMA

THE doctrines of reincarnation and *karma* offer a more satisfying explanation of the seeming inequalities and injustices of life than any other idea. It is life which is asking us to pay our past debts or is paying us for past credits.

THE purpose of reincarnation is to give the soul a better beginning in each new life, more opportunities for success, more strength to dominate the obstacles and its own failings in the pilgrimage towards its own perfection.

THE doctrine of reincarnation is that the soul has already lived on earth as man and as woman, but not as animal or plant, except before individualization, that is, before the soul became a self-conscious individual entity, never more to take birth as plant or animal.

No individual in a family comes there by mere chance, but through the working of the law of *karma*. Each person is in a family, because each is intended to help and to be helped.

THE doctrine of reincarnation, in one form or another as principle of life, has been seized upon by the intuition of man in every culture. In this principle, there are two aspects of reality: the soul which is the life, and the body which is the form. Both are interdependent, for the soul grows through experiences of the body, while the body is refined and becomes capable of greater and more true expression as the soul grows.

KARMA means action. If you do a good deed, you not only help another, but as its fruit you reap both happiness and the opportunity to create other good deeds. But if you do evil to another, you must not only pay in pain for the injury, but you belittle, make less your own nature and create a warp which you will have to remove through pain and limitation, until you are wiser and understand that evil and hatred cease only through love.

THE law of *karma* is a statement of cause and effect as a man transforms the universal energy, visible and invisible, of which he is a storehouse. That energy is beneficent and good when utilized for kindly action, but when it is employed to injure another in any way, we term it evil. We deal with the force and its effects in the spheres of action, feeling and concrete and abstract thinking.

THE Lords of *Karma* are those invisible Intelligences who administer the law of righteousness which establishes that as a man sows, so shall he reap. With infinite compassion and wisdom, but swerving not one hair's breadth from justice, They select and adjust the forces from a man's past, in new groupings that will best help him in his new incarnation.

REINCARNATION is the process of repeated births on earth, the method by which a soul grows through experiences, life after life, into wisdom, strength and beauty.

THE idea of reincarnation exists in many forms throughout the world, and the great religions are based on it. But forms of the idea which consider that individuals are sometimes reborn as animals, or have only one birth and no more, are, in the first case, a reversion and a retrogression, in the second not in accordance with occult facts, and both are contrary to the march of evolution.

Iᴛ is not the duty of the Lords of *Karma* to make a man happy or discontented, good or evil; Their one intent is so to adjust the forces of the soul's own making that his ultimate destiny shall be achieved as swiftly as may be.

Wʜɪʟᴇ the forces of past *karma* may establish one's heredity, those who help or hinder his opportunities and obligations, his physical death, they do not impose upon him the manner in which he shall *react* to them. He can react to the old *karma* and produce good rather than harmful new *karma*.

Tʜᴇ same principle of departure and return which we call reincarnation applies to every object, whether small as an atom or large as a star, whose life-history is birth, growth, maturity and decay, then return to create new atoms, stars or whatever.

THE difference between the soul who responds to an ideal and the soul who is indifferent is but a difference in experience and age as souls.

To aspire, to dream, to plan, to think, to feel, to act—all this means to set in motion forces according to the use of which we either help or hinder ourselves and others, and create *new karma* of good or ill for succeeding lives.

9. LIBERATION

THE man who has come to a true realization of his own powers can never think of utilizing them for the purpose of his own self. For he comes to that most fascinating of mysteries, that when a man realizes his own true self, he then knows it as the One Self in all that lives.

To him who has seen his archetype, no pain or disappointment can mar his enthusiasm, no heaven can entice him from its fulfilment.

THE end of the long road to liberation is in man's own heart; if only he knew it, he and the path are one.

NONE can tread the path to liberation till he knows how to create on every plane of life, in order to bring regeneration and lessen the miseries of men.

THERE are as many paths to realization and blessedness as there are souls. If, for each soul there is his own type of crucifixion, so is there also for him his particular mode of ascension.

EVERY thinking man is aware how great a mystery life is, but what he has not realized is that it brings with it its own solution; experience is the key which unlocks some part of the mystery.

WITHIN a man's own nature are inexhaustible sources of power and happiness, and every ideal which we postulate as characteristic of divinity is indeed realizable in the heart of man.

10. INTUITION

How is the intuition to be trained? By bringing to bear upon the character the forces of brotherhood and beauty. If you develop your sense of brotherhood, you will become more sensitive to beauty; if you will learn to create beauty, you will instinctively feel a sense of comradeship with all that lives.

INTUITION is acquired by no external means, but is born within a man's own heart.

So long as only the critical mental faculty functions in us, we are only a fragment of ourselves and know only a fragment of life. We shall sense the whole of ourselves only by growth in intuition, and the intuition is awakened by growing in love, by developing sensitiveness to beauty which leads to comprehension of truth and wisdom, whether in Nature or in any other sphere.

THE intuition born within a man's own inner nature gives him the sole criterion of truth, for beyond any doubt of the most critical mind he is able to know truth at first hand for himself, through impersonal observation and thinking.

IF we lay all the facts before the mind and ponder them deeply, again and again, sometimes as in a flash the intuition reveals a great truth.

THE mind divides unless completely impersonal; the intuition sees unity and not diversity, a totality throbbing with life.

THE more our natures are tender, compassionate and free from condemnation, the more likely is our intuition to manifest. A serene and kindly emotional nature often becomes the mirror of the great intuitions of the soul, who lives in a realm higher than that of the emotions.

A BEAUTIFUL way of developing intuition is by communing with Nature, being responsive to all her moods.

IN the storm and stress of any situation, the intuition sees in a flash the rightness or wrongness, the way to joy or to misery.

WHEN we become intuitive, for the first time we shall understand the potentialities of good and beauty in our own selves.

LIKE the moon in the heavens which can give a perfect image of itself on the waters of a still pond, so too when the mind is pure and the emotions are serene, the intuition can reflect its highest knowledge in our character.

IT happens occasionally that great thinkers achieve beyond their knowing—with the help of intuition, the buddhic faculty. In such a climax the intuition assembles all the thoughts into a greater, more inclusive conception which may be a new and far-reaching idea. But such an event can only occur when the higher mind, the buddhic faculty, is intensely active, where mental power and vigor provide the groundwork.

WE help ourselves and others by training our intuition, and we have an easy path, the path of love, of brotherhood, a technique of creating beauty from within.

WHEREVER the need is to understand *life* and not inert matter, it is only intuition which gives true comprehension.

THE person who streams forth goodwill, compassion and understanding becomes more and more sensitive to the beautiful in life, just as the person who links himself in brotherhood to all. When we train ourselves in true friendliness, in true attachment to life in all its phases, and particularly to the life of our fellowmen, then we grow in intuition.

JOYOUS sacrifice, a sense of renunciation, will also open the door to the intuition.

WHEREVER the community spirit is born, there is the intuitive beginning; but if there is anything coarse, crude or ugly perceived through the senses or in the environment of an individual, a twist is given to his development.

WE must trust in ourselves, and that will come as we purify our hearts and minds, and as our intuition grows.

ONE of the laws of intuition is: If once, after intuition has spoken the individual denies it in action, many an error will be his lot and much consequent suffering, before he can remove the stain from his emotional nature, so that the intuition can speak once again.

THE value of intuition is that it tells one *directly* what life is, without any intermediary or the help of any tradition of truth, such as religion or science.

INTUITION judges from *all* the facts, both from the visible and the invisible.

THE intuition is an attribute of the soul, and it is slowly coming into manifestation. It is not impulse and it is higher than the mind; it speaks only once.

ALL men are at the dawn of a new age when they will pass to the new revelation of what life is, as revealed by the intuition.

11. KNOWLEDGE

WHEN through growth in knowledge a man's mind is eagerly open to the facts which surround him, then he transmutes the knowledge gained from without into a wisdom which is part and parcel of his inmost nature.

TRUE understanding is never the result of a mere process of observation and contemplation. Action on the part of the individual is also necessary, if he would understand rightly; it is in the action which issues from him that his hidden wisdom begins to reflect itself.

WE shall discover ways in which the Divine Mind reveals Itself in the universe, not merely by seeking with the mind or even with the intuition, but we must *act* also. Unless we use the Knowledge we possess to release the divinity latent in our fellowmen, our knowledge stagnates in us and our spiritual sense becomes dull.

WITH every stage of growth into wisdom, man not only enlarges the horizon of his vision, but he embraces a vaster world in his capacity for love and sharing. To be wise is to knit into one divine Whole the ever-changing chaos of God's processes.

KNOWLEDGE ever tends to spirituality, and the wisdom which the world contains binds men of every race and creed into one indivisible Humanity.

WHEREVER we are striving to understand the Wisdom, we are assisted by the wisdom which particularly is in the living influences of Nature, even in the blades of grass.

LOVING action is Divine Wisdom at work, and whoso acts lovingly must inevitably come to the Wisdom.

12. COMPASSION

THE love of God and the love of a beloved are as the obverse and reverse of a coin; they are a unity, which in space and time are seen as a duality. There are many devotees and lovers to whom the duality still remains; only the few have transcended it.

THE love of only one must lead to the love of all before Love's true end is attained. As soon as the soul is free from the self, created by a craving to retain love, the many dimensions of love begin to be realized.

As the mind becomes purified, it becomes clear that the universe is an embodiment of Love, not only of order; it is beauty and idealism, not a passivity, but something which responds and returns love for love.

RELEASE from the lesser self begins by training oneself to grow in compassion. Compassion ever releases wisdom and strength in the soul, an intuition which understands, a strength which stands unshaken and vivifies all that is noble in the character.

THERE are many types of emotion described by the term "love," but there is only one type worthy of that name—where the loved one has, in the eyes of the lover, put on the mantle of divinity for the time being.

As immortal souls journeying to a divine fulfilment, it is our instinctive nature to love, to long for light and to seek understanding.

WE discover a little of the marvel that is man when we love him.

13. MYSTICISM

AMONG the many types of mysticism there is none first and none last; all are equally roads to God, and souls can tread equally swiftly along them all. Nor are these the only roads to Him; new mystic modes will appear as the future unfolds the hidden beauties of God's Plan of evolution.

MYSTICISM is a life of the Spirit, which cannot be held within the boundaries of any religion; it is like a mighty river which cuts out channels for itself according to its need.

To the nature mystic, the sea is the mirror of God, the sunset an open door, the mountains stand as His sentinels, the meadow, the hill and the dale, the broad expanse of field and forest, all are as the smile on His face.

MYSTICISM is as the scent of those blossoms in tropical lands, which open as the sun goes down and then perfume the air into a swooning rapture. Away from the turmoil of action, beyond where thoughts can live, the mystic senses the perfume of life, and makes his heart a chalice to gather that perfume as an offering to God and to man.

SIX types of mysticism and their related themes are: *Grace*, which affirms that the beneficence of God bridges a gulf seen between the nature of man and that of God; *Love*, with its theme of overflowing love of God towards man; *Pantheism*, which conceives God as the substratum of all things; *Nature*, in which is the all-powerful fact that the Divine Mind is mirrored in all of nature; *Sacramental*, involving ritual and ceremony by means of which the spirit of God descends directly into touch with man; and *Theosophical*, which sees the Plan of the Logos revealing itself in all the worlds and at all stages of evolution in the manifestations of the Logos.

THE mystic lives for the inner world of feeling, and his values to life in the outer world are derived from that inner world.

14. REALITY

THE reality is unfolding before our eyes age by age, and who knows what its future manifestation may be? Theosophy has discovered something, but not *everything*.

THE great reality in which our immortal natures are rooted is not far away, to be realized perhaps only after death. It is here and now, the source of every solace, as it is also the cause of all craving and death.

MEN make the greatest of mistakes in thinking that their hopes of happiness and the dreams they build are only fantasies with no substance. In reality these hopes and dreams are the first glimpses gained of the *real* world; the world of daily occupations is for us the unreal world, and when we step out of our selves, the real world steps in and we seek something which expresses the highest in us, which is a part of the divine.

To those whose eyes see only the unreal, the universe is a stage where life enters, with death at its heels in search of life. But when one perceives what is to be as the ages pass, the mystery which underlies the interaction of life and form reveals its truth.

We delude ourselves in thinking that we are now living; many of us are but as shadows flickering through life. When we can take hold of life in a real and forceful way, instead of merely looking for the meaning of life, we shall know that we ourselves are that life.

Our normal world of experience is composed of the real and the unreal, interwoven and blended. But just as it is possible in a fabric to remove either the warp or woof thread so that one remains clear and continuous, in a similar manner a trained imagination can discard the unreal in order to commune with the real.

15. TRUTH

TRUTH is known from within, with the faculty of intuition which makes one know that what is present outside is one's own, inseparable from one's own finest, inmost essence.

EVERY vision of the truth, through religion or philosophy, through science or art, or through philanthropy and service, leads the soul one step nearer to the goal, which is to live and move and have his being in full consciousness and with deep joy in the Logos of our solar system.

WITHIN men's hearts there is a longing for truth, and no soul is long content to abide in ignorance and illusion, however pleasant these may be for a time. Men desire to understand the mysteries of existence, for they know from experience that each fact discovered by them releases strength in their hearts and minds to grapple with life's problems.

Two modes of cognition of truth, in addition to the method of the mind, are the approaches of intuition and the faculties of divine spirit.

Life will never be easy for one who has within him the standard truth. For he cannot follow any tradition created by others, nor can he subscribe to their beliefs and standards which go athwart his own standard.

When we use the word "truth", we mean knowledge of the universe in all its embodiments, visible and invisible. Truth is not the result of discoveries by the seekers of truth; truth *is*, because the universe is.

We must be truthful, because truth is an ideal, and the more true we are to the facts and natural laws of life, outer and inner, the more true we are to ourselves.

IF we will only realize that not only the five senses and the mind are the avenues of perception, but also the aspirations, the imagination, our refined loves and our spirit of sacrifice, then truth will pour into our natures from many avenues now barred to us.

WHAT the senses report, what the mind perceives, what the heart conceives and the intuition knows, one or the other or all these are for men avenues to truth, according to their temperament.

16. CIVILIZATION

FROM one point of view, civilization is the discovery of as many explanations of life's mystery as possible, and the collective life of men, which we term culture, is the sum total of all the solutions gathered by their experiences.

No man exists who has not within him some little sense for beauty. It is the work of civilization to train this hidden instinct, and to make beauty a great ethical concept in the cultured man, side by side with such other concepts as sacrifice, righteousness and truth, which mold his expanding life.

No one begins to be truly educated and cultured until life is seen from a central standpoint. We are apt to miss the mark in the general activities of life when we permit divisions between our mental, emotional and moral worlds; when we thus live in compartments the results of our energies are always less forceful than they might be if we lived centered, as a whole.

We must think of civilization as the process of transforming the human into the divine.

Every truth that explains us to ourselves has an intense reality and value. All culture is a statement of discovery of the "I", and the more cultured a man is, the more he knows himself.

The rise and fall of civilizations, the growth and decay of empires, the appearances of religious teachers, law-givers, prophets and martyrs, all happen in accordance with the will of the Logos.

The sense of immortality is the crown of a great civilization.

17. BEAUTY

MAN is an agent living in worlds visible and invisible, each of which is the revelation of a consciousness and life which is Absolute Beauty. That beauty is the substance of his body, the material of his thoughts, the fabric of his imagination, and he can no more separate himself from beauty than he can separate himself from his sense of individuality.

BEAUTY has many veils, and it is only the first veil which the senses observe; they must be trained to see other veils. With each act of creation of something beautiful, the recognition of beauty increases.

BEAUTY is never static and quiescent; it is ever creative, with a mysterious quality of unfoldment, as of the bud unfolding into the flower.

THE cosmic processes of evolution are as the paints on the palette of the artist, out of which the work of art will presently issue. Behind each event, whether the birth of a star or the fading of a flower, there exists a concept, an archetype which emanates from Absolute Beauty.

THE more purified and lofty is a person's character, the more sensitive he becomes to the hidden beauty of divine manifestation in all its forms.

WE shall not know how to live truly, that is, justly and wisely, till we learn to live beautifully also.

THIS universe is not a mere mechanism, but a rhythmic life which is ever-revealing the soul of good and the heart of beauty.

WHERE beauty is perceived in all the things of life, men see that beauty, because their hearts and minds mirror the ideas as to beauty in the Divine Mind.

EVERY philosopher knows that man's capability to respond to beauty is a fundamental aspect of his character, and, therefore, no philosophy is complete which does not examine the nature of beauty.

LIGHTS and shadows, colors and forms in mineral and plant, in animal and man, are mirrors of beauty.

LOVE and you shall see the beautiful; be pure and you shall feel its power; be true and you shall know how to use that power—this is the law of the beauty which is joy.

18. UNITY

IN the theosophical conception of man, this mysterious universe is related to each individual in an intimate fashion; the beauty of the universe, the wonder of all its knowledge, cannot be dissociated from man's life. What the universe, the macrocosm, contains, man, the microcosm, unfolds. As a knowledge of the Whole explains to us the part, so too the part reveals to us the Whole.

IT is a wonderful truth that through man all life-streams flow; that the life of minerals, animals, plants, the life of the hills, streams and forests, all are in some way passing through the consciousness of each individual man.

EACH individual is bound by invisible bonds to all his fellowmen; they rise or fall with one

another. Only as he helps the whole of which he
is a part does he truly help himself. Love of one's
fellowmen and altruism in the highest form are,
therefore, the essentials of growth.

LIFE is forcing us, driving us to learn certain
lessons; and one of the great lessons is that of
the One Life, a Unity.

A WAYSIDE flower and the tiniest living creature
both throb with the message of the unity of the
cosmos.

A few anthologies available in the Quest miniature series—books for pocket or purse.

Circle of Wisdom
A Blavatsky quotation book.

Compiled by Winifred A. Parley

Short excerpts gathered together with loving care from the writings of H.P.B.

The Natural Man
A Thoreau anthology

Compiled by Robert Epstein & Sherry Phillips

Thoreau on art, life, dreams, nature, beauty, truth, solitude, self-realization, religion, friendship, sounds and silence, marriage.

Thoughts for Aspirants
By N. Sri Ram

A collection of spiritual maxims, inspirational, non-denominational, with a world view suited to today's attitudes. The author is a former President of the Theosophical Society.

All available from: Quest Books, 306 West Geneva Road, Wheaton, Illinois 60187